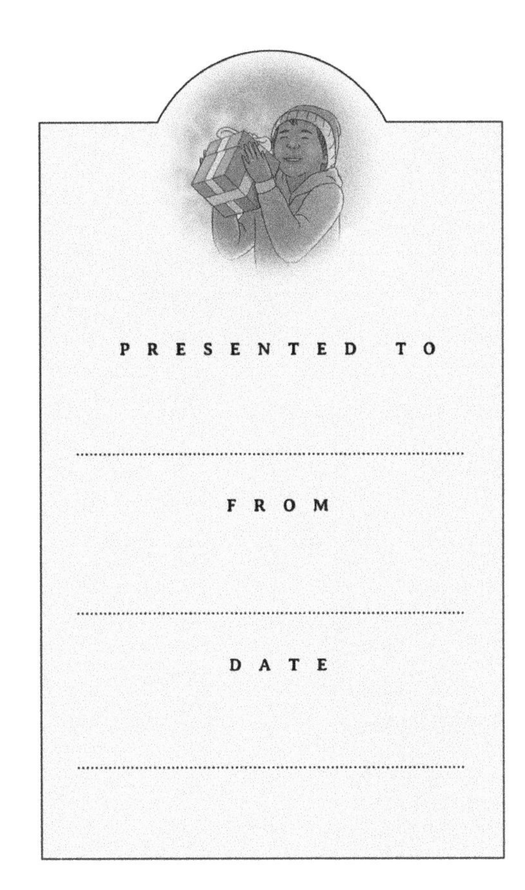

PRESENTED TO

....

FROM

....

DATE

....

To the Children of OVI Healthcare

MERRY CHRISTMAS TO ALL

Paperback ISBN: 978-1-7362243-2-8
Hardback ISBN: 978-1-7362243-8-0

OVI Healthcare, PO Box 250; Somerset, KY, 42502
www.OVIHealthcare.org
Ovi & Violet International, Inc. is a registered US 501(c)3 nonprofit organization.

MERRY CHRISTMAS *to all*

Iza Hehre

Illustrated By: **Nero Gonzaga Bernales**

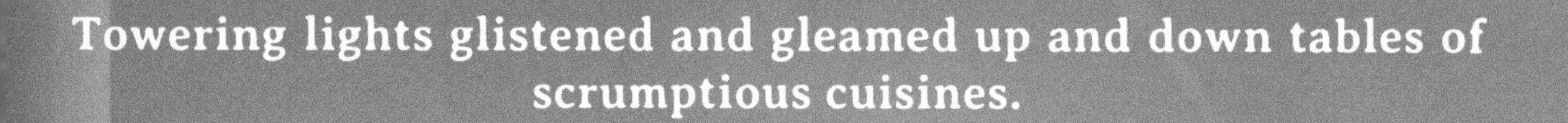

Towering lights glistened and gleamed up and down tables of scrumptious cuisines.

It was Christmas Eve dinner at Hotel La Souk, where Asa sat reading a holiday book.

That night was his mother's most difficult shift. She worked very hard, and her skill was a gift.
She washed all the dishes with speed and great care. A worker like her was incredibly rare.

But the clatter of plates and the loud conversation distracted poor Asa and caused him frustration!

"Merry..." CLACK! went the bowl... and "Merry..." SPLASH! went the sink... "Merry Christmas to all and to" BOOM! — "I can't think!!"

Asa picked up his book, walked out, and said, "That's it – I'll just stroll the lobby instead."

Away from the chaos and cold marble floors, Asa waltzed into the grand corridors.

The decadent lobby, a sight to behold, was even far greater than what he'd been told.

He strolled past the Christmas trees, humming a carol. He breathed in the sweetness

of treats by the barrel!
Best of all, Asa thought, after tonight, I’ll open my presents with joy and delight!

He circled about the immense celebration until he saw Kai at the trolley station.

"Kai!" Asa shouted. He rushed down the block, but the building doors shut, and the keypad was locked.

He sighed in dismay – then a great twist of fate! – the door swung wide open. “Come in, child, it’s late!”

He paused and then said, “There’s a party inside?” He wasn’t invited, no time to decide!

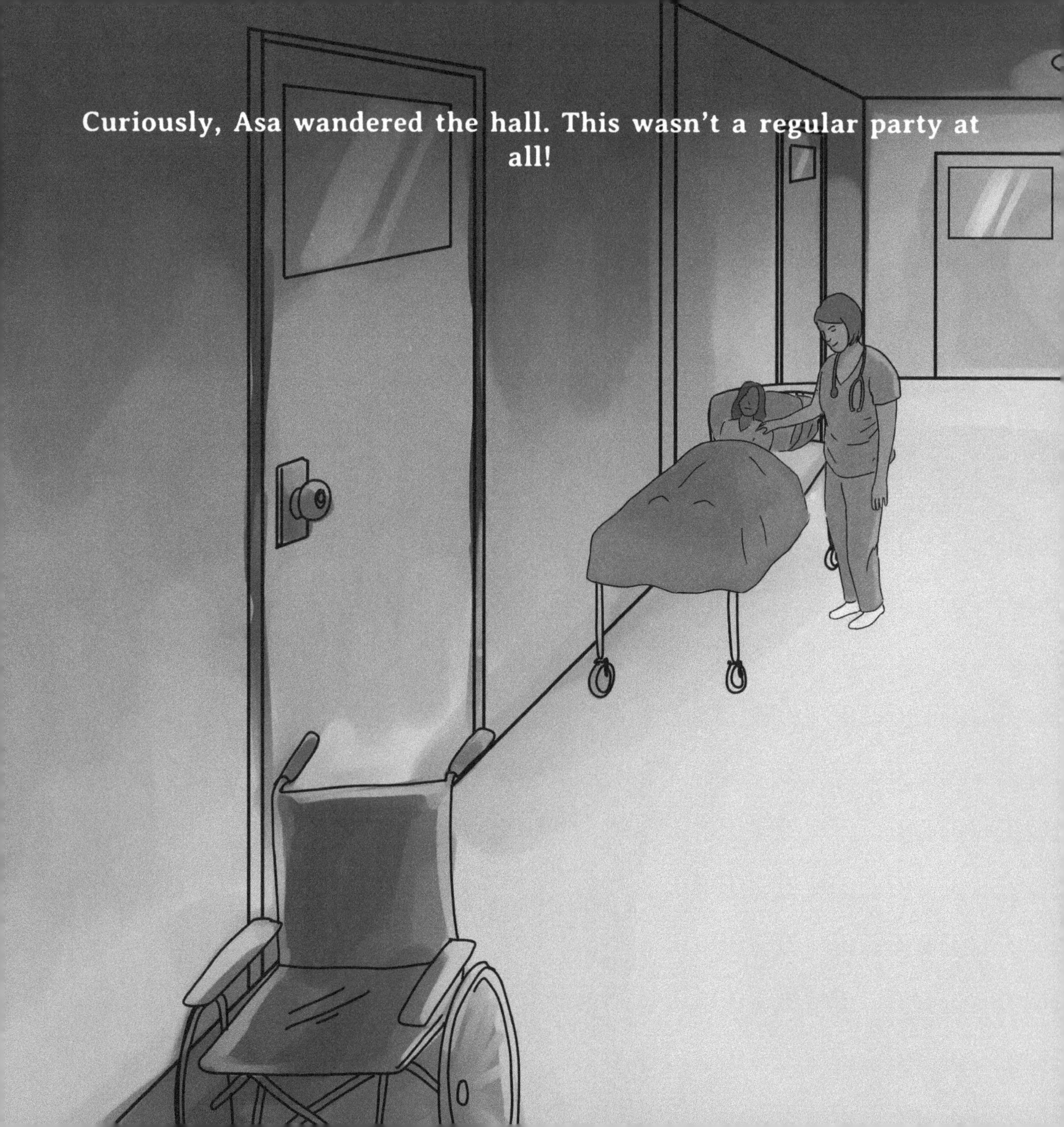

Curiously, Asa wandered the hall. This wasn't a regular party at all!

A boy named Elias was eating green pea mash because he couldn't safely swallow his Christmas treat stash.

Then there was Nelly and a story of reindeer, but someone read the book in a language she couldn't hear.

Next, Manu was seated beside a sparkling tree, but it wasn't special for him because Manu couldn't see.

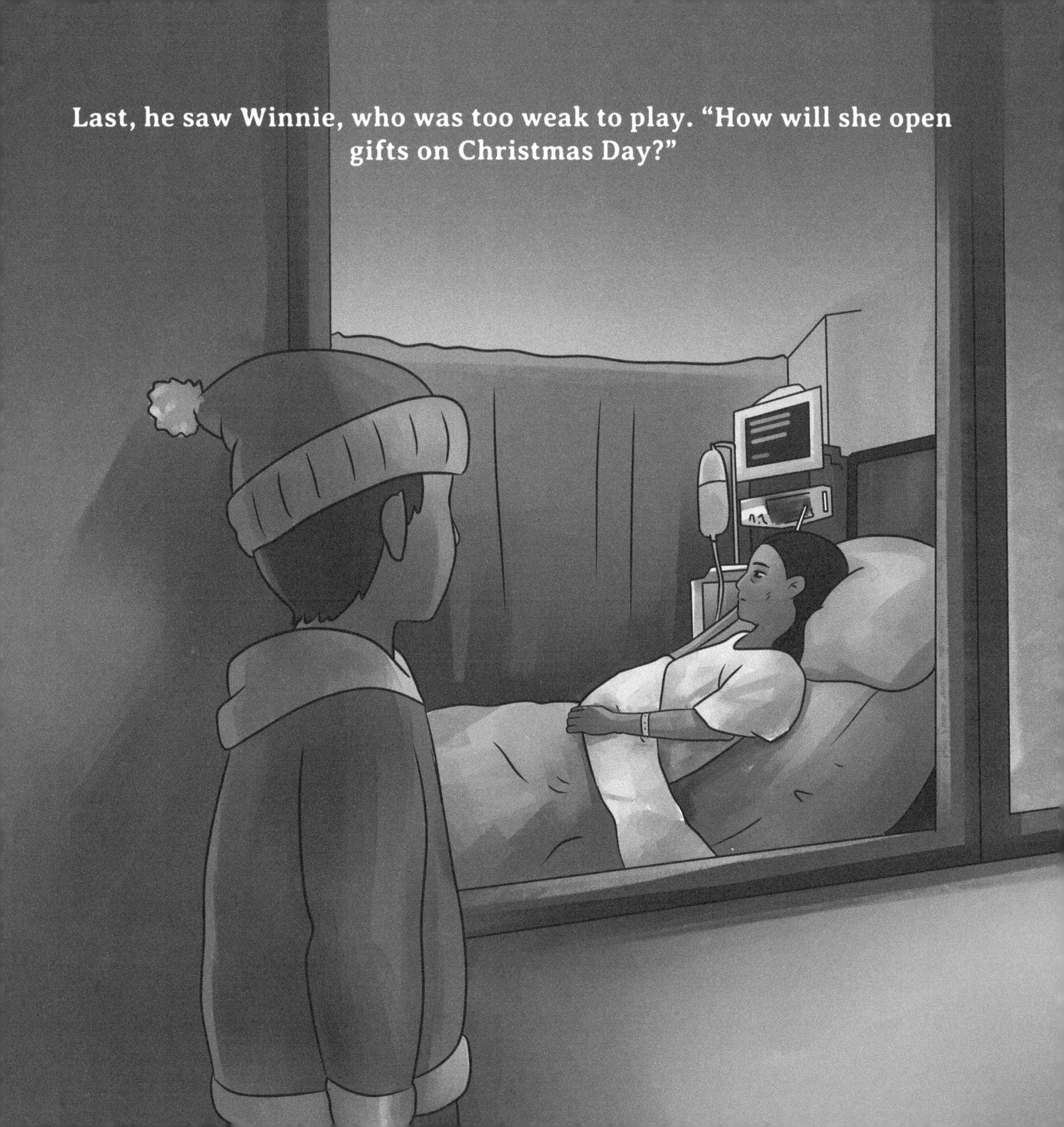

Last, he saw Winnie, who was too weak to play. “How will she open gifts on Christmas Day?”

Then something struck him, a line from his books. “Merry Christmas to all” is much more than it looks!

Our celebrations don’t always consider Elias, Winnie, Nelly, or Manu. But oh, don’t you see? They want a “Merry Christmas” too!”

Their hearts are so big and should be packed full of joy. They deserve all the cheer and a thoughtful toy.

It's holiday wisdom we can't ever lose: A Merry Christmas is a choice you must choose!

أحبُ المساعدة

And so, Asa felt inspired, and his calling was clear. He'd bring a Merry Christmas to ALL this very year!

The End

MERRY CHRISTMAS *to all*

Draw a line from the child to the special gift they received.
Then discuss why that present was perfect for their unique need.

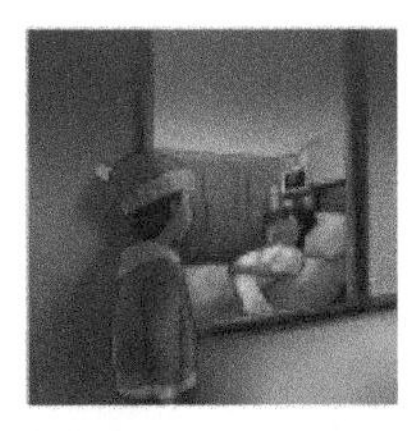

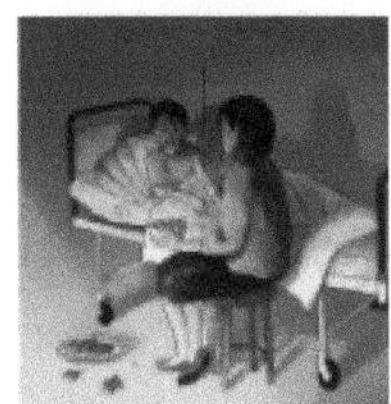

MERRY CHRISTMAS *to all*

Answer Key

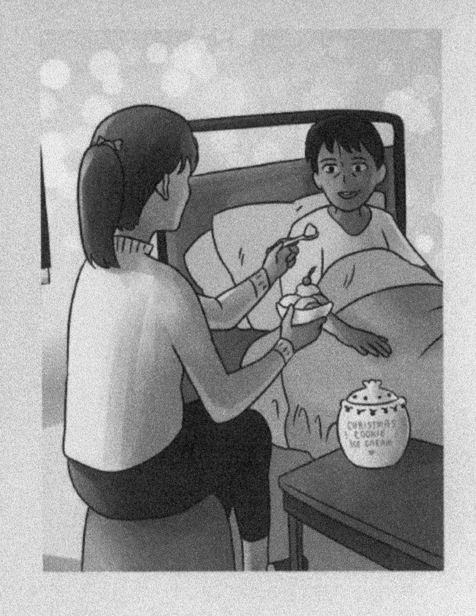

Elias struggles with holiday treats you must chew, but with Christmas cookie ice cream he smiles with every spoon!

Winnie was too weak to go out and play, but her new dog Snowball snuggles beside her all day!

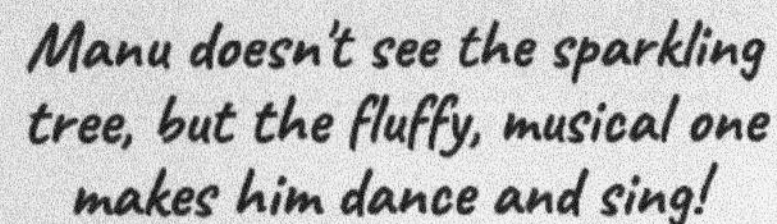

Manu doesn't see the sparkling tree, but the fluffy, musical one makes him dance and sing!

Nelly didn't understand the story she heard, but with her new books, she can read every word!

Kai couldn't safely climb to hang the star on the tree, but now – with his drone, he can reach everything!

Life-changing healthcare for the world's most vulnerable children.

100% of proceeds from this book provide critical medical services to orphaned, abandoned, and vulnerable children who would otherwise have no access to care.

To learn more, follow @OVIHealthcare on social media and visit **www.OVIHealthcare.org.**

CPSIA information can be obtained
at www.ICGtesting.com
Printed in the USA
LVHW071230141220
674128LV00003B/31